LITTLE BIRD

By J.M. Walsh

This book is a work of fiction. Names, characters, places, and incidents are products of the author's imagination or are used fictitiously. Any resemblance to actual events, locales, or persons, living or dead, is entirely coincidental.

Breakthrough Publishers is an imprint of Breakthrough Change Management Ltd.

www.breakthroughchange.com

ISBN (Paperback): 978-1-9193918-3-0

ISBN (eBook): 978-1-9193918-4-7

Story and text by J.M. Walsh

Illustrations by Hayley Trampenau

First Edition: 2026

Printed in the United Kingdom.

For Kay,
who makes all
flights possible.

Table of Contents

CHAPTER ONE

The Edge of the Branch

It began on a morning when the mist stayed low.

Little Bird stood where the birch branch thinned to nothing. Below, the meadow lay drowned in white. Above was the sun hidden by clouds. Behind him, the nest of twigs, feathers, hours of labour. Ahead, only air.

He lifted one foot. The wind touched it, curious and cool. He set it back down.

He'd been there since dawn. The others had already gone some graceful, some tumbling, all landing clumsily and alive.

His mother had told him every morning that his wings were perfect strong, full, ready. But when he spread them now, they trembled.

The air pressed against his feathers, cool and certain, testing its hold.

He stepped back. The nest creaked behind him.

Bee hadn't planned to be here. She was meant to be on a gathering run the kind the Queen sent older bees whose wings had frayed, whose stings had dulled, whose stories had outlived their use. Everyone knew such errands weren't necessary. No one said so.

She flew slower than she once did, pausing often, pretending to examine flowers so the younger bees wouldn't see how the wind moved her. She took a long detour to the clover patches and didn't admit, even to herself, why.

Then something quivered in the mist, feathers jerking the way they do when a body wants to run but doesn't.

A small bird, alone on a branch. Bee knew that kind of loneliness.

She hovered, curious. Her missions had become chores, but this was different unexpected.

She settled on a nearby leaf, sting tucked away, wings resting. Then drifted nearer.

"Trying?" she asked, her voice carrying the roughness of too many seasons.

Little Bird turned, startled. The old bee hovered beside the branch stripes faded, hum low and steady, smelling faintly of damp meadow.

"I was… I am…" Little Bird stopped.

"Good," said Bee, landing on the branch. "What shall I call you?"

"I'm Little Bird," he said, though he sounded smaller than the words.

"Bee," said Bee, and smiled with her hum.

They stood together without speaking. Below them, birds chased each other through the branches as if nothing had happened.

Bee nodded toward the nest. "Getting here is something."

Little Bird blinked. He had thought 'something' belonged to birds who were already flying, those who sliced the sky and didn't wobble. He had not considered that hopping to the edge might count.

"The wind is strong," said Little Bird, as if it were an explanation for everything.

"It is," Bee agreed. "And still, here you are."

Little Bird's voice dropped. "My brother wasn't afraid of the wind. It took him."

Bee's hum faltered a small skip in the air. "Oh," she said quietly.

Little Bird nodded, eyes fixed on the white-covered meadow where his brother's body had fallen, small, broken and still.

Bee shifted, her wings trembled. "I'm sorry," she said.

The silence that followed was long.

"You're still here," she said.

Little Bird winced, and her antennae drooped.

They stood together, not close, not touching, looking out across the place where falling and flying start from the same step.

"So, you see," Little Bird said, steadier now, "what if I'm right to be afraid. What if the voice that says stay is the one that keeps you alive?"

Bee said nothing for a moment, just watched.

They looked out together. Mist lifted in small breaths. A spider's web beaded the light. Nothing urgent happened.

"May I ask you something?" Bee said.

Little Bird braced. "If it's troublesome, perhaps you could ask it quietly."

Bee's hum softened. "How would you know you're ready?"

Little Bird tilted his head, considering. "It would feel sure. Like the wind is gentle. Like you can't fall. Like everyone else was born knowing how."

A pair of swallows shot past overhead, writing fast sentences across the air.

"They make it look easy," Bee said. "But they've all fallen."

Little Bird watched the swallows. They made it look effortless, cutting through the air like it was nothing, as if they'd been born knowing the language. But that wasn't the whole story. They'd stood on branches too, once.

They were quiet long enough to hear the birch tell its creak-story to the morning. Somewhere below, a water vole stitched a neat line along the streambank. A day, unremarkable, gently unfolding.

"I thought I had to feel different first," Little Bird admitted. "Before I could try."

Bee chuckled, low and warm. "The sky doesn't wait. Eventually, the flock leaves."

Little Bird looked down, claws curling tight around the branch. "I know."

"How long?" Bee asked gently.

"Mother says when the last blackberries soften. Maybe a little after, if the winds stay warm."

His gaze followed the curve of the valley to the pale horizon. Far beyond, wings were already gathering in shifting shapes he did not yet belong to. The long flight south. The one every bird made. Some did not survive.

"The others are already flying together," Little Bird murmured. His wings folded tight.

Bee shifted her weight. The hum in her chest changed.

"This branch," she said slowly. "We could start here."

Little Bird stared at the valley. "What if I can't?"

Bee didn't answer immediately. She was looking at something in the grass below a feather, white and delicate, caught on a stem. One of Little Bird's down feathers, probably lost during preening. It trembled in the breeze but didn't fall.

"See that?" Bee said, pointing.

Little Bird followed her gaze.

"The feather held."

Bee moved closer along the branch, and Little Bird noticed for the first time how carefully she walked, how her legs trembled slightly with each step

"Would you like to try something? Small."

Little Bird's stomach tightened. "...Small enough not to fall?"

"Open your wings," Bee said quietly. "Just open them. Let the wind meet them for a moment."

Little Bird looked at her doubtfully. "That's not flying."

Bee's wings flickered. "It's a start."

The wind picked up slightly, making the branch sway. Little Bird's claws dug harder into the bark. Every part of him said hold.

"I can't," he whispered.

Bee's antennae dipped slightly. Listening quietly.

"My brother" Little Bird's voice caught. "He opened his wings, and the wind took him."

Bee said nothing for a moment. Then, she said, "You're you."

Little Bird stood frozen, breathing fast. Then his wings began to open.

The air immediately found them, sliding between feathers, lifting slightly at the edges. Little Bird felt the wind holding a fraction of him, even here.

He looked down. The ground was still far below. But his wings his wings were meeting air, it didn't fight him it spoke, softly, in currents.

"Oh," he whispered.

He folded his wings again, slowly, feeling how they moved.

Bee said nothing, simply watching, her hum quieter than before.

“Thank you,” Little Bird said finally.

Bee’s antennae dipped. “I should be thanking you,” she said. “The hive gave me a route that doesn’t matter. Flowers that don’t need gathering. But this” She looked at Little Bird, and for the first time her age showed in her eyes, not just her wings. “This mattered.”

“I’ll be here tomorrow,” Little Bird said.

“So will I,” Bee said.

They sat together as the morning grew warmer. Two creatures who had found each other by chance.

The sun broke through the clouds, sending light streaming across the valley. Everything shimmered wet leaves, spider silk, the distant river.

Bee stirred, stretching her legs one at a time. “Tomorrow,” Bee said, rising into the air.

"Will it feel the same?"

"I don't know," Bee said. "That's worth finding out."

She flew toward the meadow, slower than she had in her youth, but steady. Little Bird watched her go, this old bee who had set aside her own errands to sit with a frightened bird.

When Bee was out of sight, Little Bird stretched out his wings again, just to see. The air wasn't exactly as before it carried a new charge, as though excited for him but it stayed steady. It didn't matter that he hadn't jumped.

He folded them again and looked out at the valley, where the flock would soon gather, where the sky stretched on forever in every direction.

He didn't fly that morning. He had started anyway.

CHAPTER TWO

The Branch Below

The next morning arrived with dew still heavy on the branches.

Little Bird waited on the same branch where the air had first lifted him. He had slept lightly, dreaming of endless sky and a voice that whispered, "You can." When he opened his eyes, Bee was already there, suspended as though the night had simply paused around her.

"You've woken early," said Bee.

"I didn't want the wind to change without me," said Little Bird.

Bee chuckled, low and warm. "Wind always changes. We just learn to move with it."

They sat together as the light crept between the leaves. The morning tasted clean, like rain that hadn't fallen yet.

"I did what you said," Little Bird began. "I opened my wings yesterday. And the air answered."

"I could tell," Bee said. "You're holding yourself differently."

Little Bird tilted his head, considering. "It was only a small thing."

Bee landed beside Little Bird, settling her weight carefully.

They watched the valley wake, mist lifting, calls filling the air, the day unfolding slowly before them.

"Were you ever afraid?" Little Bird asked suddenly. "Of flying?"

Bee's hum changed pitch. "Terrified. My first long flight I was so frightened I couldn't feel my legs. Kept trying to turn back, but the older bees nudged me on. 'Just the next flower,' they'd say. By the time we landed, I'd passed so many flowers we could have stopped at."

Little Bird tried to picture this old bee, so sure now, shaking in the air.

"What changed?"

"Nothing changed," Bee said. "I just kept flying until I'd done it enough times to remember I could do it."

There was a pause, not empty but filled with thought.

Below them, a younger bird hopped along a lower branch, testing its wings in short, uneven flaps. It jumped, dropped a few inches, flailed, caught itself, then tried again without pause.

"Did you see that?" Little Bird asked. "It failed and just kept going."

"Was it supposed to stop?" Bee asked.

Little Bird opened his beak, then shut it again, thinking. "Maybe… maybe not." He looked away. "I used to be like that… before my brother."

Bee was quiet. "He tried," she said at last.

Little Bird glanced down at the lower branch again. Then at Bee. Then at the branch.

"Will you..." He couldn't finish.

"I'll be right here," Bee said.

No one had said that to him since his brother. His mother had said she loved him, that he was strong, that he was ready. But she hadn't said she'd stay. She had her own flights to think about, her own survival. She couldn't wait forever for a little bird who might never jump.

But this old bee had nowhere else she needed to be. Not right now.

He leaned forward. The lower branch looked farther away now, not closer. His breath came short. His wings started to open without permission an old reflex, preparing for flight even though he wasn't flying, just stepping down.

"Not yet," he told his wings. "Not yet."

He bent his legs. The branch beneath his feet was solid, known, safe. The branch below was unknown territory lower, yes, but also different. New bark. New angle.

His back foot slipped not far, just enough to throw his weight forward and suddenly he was dropping, wings snapping open too late, crashing onto the lower branch in a knot of feathers and breath.

His claws scrabbled. Caught. Held.

He was down.

He stood there, breath coming fast, wings still spread wide like he might need them any second, looking up at where he'd been.

"That wasn't the neatest landing," Bee said, floating down beside him.

Little Bird's laugh surprised them both, sharp and breathless. "I fell."

"You did," Bee agreed. "But you're also on a new branch. So, what do we call that?"

Little Bird looked around. The meadow looked different from here closer somehow. He could now see individual flowers, not just a blur of colour. A beetle was navigating a grass stem with the kind of determined patience that suggested it had been doing this for a long time and would continue longer again, oblivious to birds and bees and their small dramas.

A spider was repairing its web in the space between two branches, leg testing each strand, silk catching light.

The web had been broken something large had flown through, probably but the spider didn't pause in the damaged place. It simply rebuilt, one strand at a time.

The nest above looked smaller than it had. Not gone. Just... less everything.

Little Bird smiled. "A start?"

But Bee nodded as if Little Bird had said something profound. "A start, yes."

They stayed on the new branch while the sun climbed higher and the mist burned off completely. Little Bird tested his grip, shifted his weight, spread his wings and folded them again. Everything was different from down here. Not better or worse. Just different.

The air moved differently against his feathers. The tree creaked in a different register lower, more grounded. Even his own heartbeat sounded different.

He could move. He could choose a direction even if he didn't know where it led.

"In the hive," Bee said quietly, "there's a wall by the entrance rough, etched with tiny scratches. An old bee once told me each mark was a storm, a day the hive thought it wouldn’t survive.” Her hum softened. “She touched the deepest one. ‘That was my first winter,’ she said. ‘I was sure we’d die. But spring came anyway.’“

Little Bird looked at the branch beneath his feet, at the nest behind him. How many storms had they already survived?

“Funny how we forget the cold nights once the sun’s back,” Bee said.

Little Bird spread his wings briefly, testing. They’d steadied him in the fall without being asked. His claws had found the branch without thinking. His body had been keeping score of things his mind forgot.

“Tomorrow,” Bee said. “We’ll see what the morning brings.”

Little Bird didn’t answer. He looked down at the next branch, then down past that to the dozens of branches between here and the ground.

So many small falls before the big one.

“Tomorrow,” he agreed.

Above them, the empty branch swayed, already forgetting he'd been there.

Below them, the meadow waited, patient as always.

And Little Bird stood on a new branch, learning what it was like to be somewhere he'd chosen instead of somewhere he'd always been.

CHAPTER THREE

The Quiet between the Wings

That night, the forest whispered.

Little Bird tucked his head beneath his wing, but sleep wouldn't come. The nest that was safe at dusk now seemed exposed, every rustle below a fox, every shadow overhead an owl. His mother slept beside him, breathing the slow rhythm of the unafraid.

Why couldn't he feel like that?

The voices arrived instead.

You're not ready.

What if you fall?

Everyone else has flown already.

He shifted on the branch, trying to make his body forget what his mind remembered. Below, a mouse rustled through last year's leaves, sure of its path. Even the mouse knew its way in the darkness.

Little Bird pulled his head out from under his wing and stared at the stars. They were so far away they didn't even know he existed, and somehow that made him feel smaller.

The voices swelled. His body braced hard beneath his ribs.

Then

A soft hum. Wings that never hurried.

"You're awake," said Bee.

Little Bird's heart jumped. "I was trying not to be."

Bee settled on the branch without question, folding her wings slowly. For a while, they simply sat. The night breathed wind in leaves, distant water, and old wood creaking as the air cooled.

Little Bird waited for something words, a hum, a sign but Bee only watched the dark.

At last, Little Bird whispered, "They won't stop."

"Mm?"

"The voices." His own voice came out smaller than he meant. "They keep telling me I'll fall. That I'll make a fool of myself." He paused, then said the thing he'd been thinking all evening, the thing that made his stomach hurt: "That I'm just not meant to fly."

Bee's antennae lowered in recognition.

"What do they sound like?" Bee asked.

Little Bird closed his eyes. "Like my mother, but worried. Like my brother, who warned me. And like me, only meaner. Like I'm the thing to be afraid of."

The moon filtered through the canopy above, turning everything silver in broken patches of light.

"What would you tell another bird," Bee asked, "if they were afraid to fly?"

Little Bird frowned. "I'd tell them everyone falls at first. Even swallows."

"Would you tell them they're not meant to fly?"

"No."

Bee said nothing. The wind moved through the leaves.

Little Bird looked at her in the moonlight. "But I don't think I can."

"No," Bee said. "Not yet."

They sat for a while. The voices hadn't gone, but they'd drifted outward, like clouds sliding towards the horizon. The tightness in his chest had loosened just enough to let a full breath in.

She drifted away into the dark, her hum fading until it was just another sound the forest made at night.

Little Bird tucked his head beneath his wing. The voices were still there not sharp now, more like words running out of breath. And beneath them, very faint: *Tomorrow.*

It didn't sound like Bee. It didn't sound like his mother or his brother. It sounded, impossibly, like him.

Morning came with light.

Little Bird woke to find the world edged in gold, each blade of grass holding a trembling bead of dew. The warmth made everything clearer, sounds travelled softly but true, scents drifted sweeter.

Bee arrived as the sun burned pink across the valley.

"Today," Bee said, settling on the branch, "we're not going anywhere."

Little Bird's shoulders dropped. "We're not?"

"No. Today, we see what your wings know."

The branch was slippery. Little Bird adjusted his grip, claws finding purchase in the rough bark. His wings shifted automatically balancing, compensating, adjusting his weight without being asked.

"See?" Bee said. "You just did it."

Little Bird looked at his own wings as if seeing them for the first time. They were still folded, but they'd moved. Small adjustments. The kind of thing bodies do when minds aren't paying attention.

"Open them," Bee said softly.

Little Bird hesitated. Then opened his wings halfway. The cold air pressed against his feathers, sliding through the gaps, finding the spaces.

"More."

Little Bird opened them fully. The wind caught them immediately, pressing upward, trying to lift him off the branch. His feet gripped harder.

"Feel that?" Bee asked.

"The wind."

"The lift."

Little Bird held his wings open, feeling the steady pressure. It was strong stronger than he'd expected. Not violent, just persistent. Like something patient who would wait as long as needed but wouldn't stop offering.

His shoulders burned. His back ached. But the wind kept pressing upward.

"How long?" Little Bird asked, voice tight.

"Until they have to fold."

Little Bird held on. His wings trembled with the strain. The muscles along his back ached. His chest heaved. But he held.

He kept them open until his wings folded on their own.

He stood there, breath coming fast, the echo of the lift still alive in his body.

“They hurt,” he said.

“They worked,” Bee said.

They sat in the warming morning, watching clouds reshape themselves over the valley. Little Bird had been trying to explain something about how watching other birds made everything worse, not better but the words weren’t cooperating.

“They make it look like nothing,” Little Bird said finally. “Like the air just holds them up.”

Bee’s hum dropped lower. “The air doesn’t want anything. It just is. And they’ve all fallen before. Every one of them.”

“Not like I will.”

“No,” Bee said. “Probably differently. But still falling.”

Little Bird’s head tilted. “Did you? Fall?”

Bee was quiet for so long that Little Bird thought she wouldn’t answer. The silence stretched, filled with things unsaid and memories that still hurt even when held carefully.

Then the old bee's wings shifted, settling into a different position.

"I wasn't always slow," Bee said finally. Her voice had changed, somehow becoming smaller. "I was fast once. Fastest in my hatching group. The Queen gave me important missions deep meadow runs, the clover patches past the stream where the honey buzzards hunt. Other bees got lost out there. I never did."

She paused.

"I got proud," Bee continued. "Stopped checking the sky. Stopped listening to the warnings. I knew better, you see. I was fast. I was good. The rules were for slower bees, not for me."

Little Bird waited.

"There was a young bee. New to the gathering flights." Bee's wings drooped. "She asked to come with me one day. The winds kept changing direction; the honey buzzards were hunting early every sign said stay close to the hive. But she looked at me like I could make things safe just by being there. Like my speed was the same as safety. So, I said yes."

The hum in Bee's chest had gone rough, unsteady.

"We got separated. I'd flown too far ahead, probably showing off, or just not paying attention the way I should have. I heard her alarm call. High. Thin. Like the air itself screaming."

Little Bird's claws curled tight into the bark. He wanted Bee to stop talking but also needed her to continue.

"I flew toward it, but I was too far. Too far, too late, and too stupid to have prevented it in the first place. The honey buzzard got her while I watched from the flowers. Couldn't do anything. Too small, too slow, too late. She was gone before I could even reach her."

The silence that followed had weight, as if it were pressing down on the branch between them.

"I went back to the hive," Bee said. "Told the Queen what happened. She didn't punish me. But I couldn't fly fast after that."

She turned to look at Little Bird directly, antennae forward, eyes holding something raw and unhealed.

“The other bees think I’m old, worn out, past my prime. And maybe I am. But the truth is, I’ve been slow for years, ever since that day. I’m not slow because my body has failed. I’m slow because I’m afraid I’ll get someone killed again. So, I fly carefully. So careful, I only fly to nearby flowers now.”

Little Bird’s voice came out smaller. “Is that why you stopped? For me?”

“Yes,” Bee said simply.

Bee was still flying slower now, wings frayed but sure.

“Do you still hear her?” Little Bird asked.

“Every day,” Bee said. “But softer now. Some mornings I think she’d understand.”

Little Bird was quiet for a moment. “You miss her,” he said.

Bee’s antennae lifted slightly. “I do. And I still think of the day I didn’t turn back soon enough.” She gave a small, uneven hum. “A bee can’t unmake honey once it’s stored. You only choose which flower to fly too next. So, I chose the slower ones. Closer ones. Ones that felt safe."

Little Bird looked at her. "Maybe that's both fear and care."

Bee smiled, faint and true. "Maybe both."

"You're here," Little Bird said. "You stopped for me. You didn't have to."

Bee nodded slowly.

They sat together as the day warmed around them. The sun climbed higher. The meadow woke wings, whiskers, and quiet hunger moving through the grass.

That afternoon, the other young birds circled overhead, calling to each other across the canopy. Showing off. Comparing distances.

"I made it to the oak!" one called.

"I flew across the stream!" another answered.

"Watch this!" a third shouted, diving, pulling up, looping back around all grace and confidence and terrifying ease.

Little Bird looked away, claws pressing into the branch.

You're the only one left who can't do this.

"They're loud," Little Bird said, nodding toward the young flock.

"They're performing for each other," Bee said.

Below, two bees hovered near a patch of clover. Little Bird watched them face each other. Their hums rose sharply. One gestured toward the south field, the other toward the shadowed grove.

Little Bird held his breath, already bracing for the sting.

But they paused, circled once, and flew back toward the hive together.

"I couldn't do that," he said quietly. "When I'm upset, I fold in."

Bee's antennae lowered. "Many creatures do."

"Isn't it safer?"

Bee was quiet for a moment.

The quiet settled heavily in his chest.

Little Bird didn't move all the swallowed words, all the things he hadn't said to his mother, to the other birds, even to himself.

A gust of wind carried the scent of honey up from below, warm and golden.

"Would you like to see?" Bee asked.

Little Bird leaned forward. "See the hive?"

"If you'd like."

Little Bird looked at the distance. It wasn't far, but farther than he'd gone since that first descent. His claws curled instinctively.

Then a soft downy feather, one of his own, lifted free in the breeze and spiralled lazily toward the meadow below.

"Then we'll take the long way," Bee said. "Hop, climb, walk."

So, they went.

Branch by branch, Little Bird descended. When he reached the lowest branch, he paused, looking down at the grass that came up to his chest.

"You did that," Bee said. "Every branch, a choice."

Little Bird dropped to the ground a short hop that landed solid. The earth was different from bark. More certain. Less willing to sway.

They crossed the meadow, Bee in slow arcs, Little Bird hopping through clover. The hive grew larger, golden and alive with sound.

Then Little Bird saw them.

Two bees were at the entrance, facing each other. One older, wings frayed. One younger, bright and quick. The younger bee's hum rose not aggressive, but urgent.

The older bee's hum was lower, slower, cautious, resistant.

But the young bee didn't back down. Her hum wasn't louder, but clearer somehow, like light through clean water.

The older bee's antennae drooped. He shifted aside.

The young bee touched his wing gently as she passed and disappeared into the hive.

"She asked for rest time," Bee said.

"She looked so tiny," Little Bird whispered.

"She was," Bee agreed. "But her voice wasn't."

They stood in the hive's shadow, the scent of wax and honey wrapping them in heat and life. Around them, bees came and went some in pairs, some alone.

"Bee," he said carefully, testing the words in his mouth, "sometimes when you talk, you explain so much I can't hear my own thoughts."

The words hung in the air between them.

Bee went very still. Her wings stopped mid-beat for just a fraction of a second. Then she settled on a stone, and Little Bird saw something vulnerable cross her face.

"You're right," Bee said finally, voice softer than Little Bird had ever heard it. "Thank you for saying it."

Little Bird's feathers felt warm. Not shame, but something else.

"I didn't hurt you?" he asked.

Bee smiled. "It stung my pride, but pride mends." She looked at Little Bird with something that might have been respect. "You gave me honesty."

Little Bird breathed out, feeling suddenly lighter, as if words that had been living under his feathers had finally found air.

"The day they moved me to the closed flowers," Bee said, "I said nothing. Just nodded. Smiled, even. Went home and sat in the dark for three days."

"What would you have said?" Little Bird asked.

Bee thought for a moment. "I'm slowing down, and that frightens me. I still have so much to give. Please don't stop hearing me." She smiled sadly. "Simple words. But I never found them in time."

"I'm glad you found me," Little Bird whispered.

Bee's hum warmed. "So am I."

They made the climb back in easy silence, Bee looping above, Little Bird steady on bark and breath. The voices in his head were still there *you're too slow, you're not ready, everyone else is better* but quieter somehow. Or maybe just less important than the voice he'd found today, the one that could speak its own kind of honesty.

When they reached the branch, Bee settled beside him.

Little Bird spread his wings again. Held them open. The wind was offering its steady upward press.

This time, he held for a long time before the ache became too much.

When he folded them, Bee nodded. "You held it."

Little Bird looked at his wings these things that knew what to do even when he didn't, that practised while he worried, that held him on the branch and would someday hold him in the air.

"They're not perfect," Little Bird said.

"No," Bee agreed. "But they're yours. And they're learning."

They sat until the day was fully itself warm, bright, indifferent to their small struggles and smaller victories.

When Bee finally rose to leave, her hum sounded different somehow. Not lighter, exactly. But less alone.

"Tomorrow," she said, "we'll try feeling different kinds of wind."

"There are different kinds?" Little Bird asked.

"Many," Bee said. "And your wings already know most of them."

She lifted off, hovered for a moment, then drifted back toward the meadow, where flowers waited, work continued, and the hive hummed with its quiet purpose.

Little Bird watched her go, then looked at his own wings again.

The wings didn't answer. But they were there, folded and ready, waiting for the moment when head and body would finally speak the same language and step off the branch together.

Not today. But someday.

Little Bird could feel it now not as certainty, but as possibility.

CHAPTER FOUR

The Clumsy Sky

Morning began with a wind that had something to say.

It rushed through the birch leaves, tugging their silver undersides until the whole tree shimmered. Little Bird was already awake, pacing the branch. His feathers caught the light differently sharper, each one holding its shape.

Bee arrived with an excited hum.

"You've been waiting," she said.

"I have," said Little Bird. "I'm just not sure for what."

Bee landed beside him, setting down a sun-sparked drop of nectar. "A little something for energy."

He sipped; sweetness spread through him. It tasted of summer and distant flowers, of places he hadn't been but might reach.

"All night the thought kept circling," Little Bird said. "About yesterday. When I spoke up."

"Yes?"

"It was good," he admitted. "Scary. But good."

They watched the meadow wake. Dew was heavy, each blade wearing its own small mirror. A fox moved below, quick and purposeful.

"How does the fox know where to step?" Little Bird asked.

"He knows the ground," Bee said. "He's walked it often."

Little Bird watched the fox disappear into the undergrowth. "I want that," he whispered. "That certainty."

"Looks sure," Bee said, "Maybe it's just hungry enough to try. Or maybe it simply keeps moving."

Wind picked up, swaying the branch. Little Bird's wings extended for balance before he noticed.

"See?" Bee said. "Your wings move faster than your mind."

Little Bird looked at his wings, still extended, making tiny adjustments. "I'm balancing. Not flying."

"Same wings, though." Said Bee.

A young swallow shot past overhead blur and whistle.

"Ready to try?" Bee asked.

Little Bird edged forward. The air was different today. His toes curled over the bark's edge. He looked down at the branch below the one he'd hopped to before.

"That one?" Bee asked.

"That one." He nodded to a lower branch not too far away.

Bee went still. "That's farther."

"I know," Little Bird said. "But I think... I think I need to try."

He practised where he was… drop, catch, land. Again, and again. Then he froze at the edge.

"What's wrong?" Bee asked.

Little Bird stared at the distance below. "My brother," he said quietly.

For a long time, neither spoke. The wind moved through the leaves. Below them, life continued oblivious.

"Different," Bee said finally. "Not his path. Yours."

"What if there is no safe path?"

"There isn't," Bee said. "But there are paths you choose with your eyes open."

Little Bird looked at the branch below. Not the ground. Not the highest point. Somewhere in between.

"He was trying to be brave," Little Bird whispered.

"And he taught you something," Bee said. "Not what to do. What not to do."

Little Bird spread his wings slightly, feeling the wind test them. "I'm not being reckless," he said.

"No," Bee agreed. "You're not."

Bee's face shifted, approval, sadness, hope. "Then try," she said. "I'm here."

Little Bird spread his wings. Morning air filled them. Wind moved through his feathers, shaping them. His stomach tightened.

He looked at the branch below. Saw claws finding bark, gripping. Saw himself landing.

"Step off," he told himself. "Your wings will remember."

Little Bird stepped off.

For one perfect moment, it held. The air caught him. He was gliding, down and forward. Wind under each feather, tail trimming course. His body knew this. His wings had been practising this every time they balanced, every time they spread.

Then his mind caught up.

"You're flying, wait, what if you" whispered a voice in his head.

His wings lost rhythm. His body tensed. Glide became tumble.

The branch rushed up too fast, coming at him sideways. He tried to correct. A wing clipped a twig. He spun. Claws raked bark, found nothing. Wings thrashed.

For a moment, he had it. His claws found bark, started to grip.

Slipped.

He fell through leaves and tugged twigs. His shoulder hit a fork in the branches, and breath fled. He scrambled wildly until claws caught and held.

He clung there, halfway down, gasping. His wing throbbed where it had clipped. His shoulder burned. Worse was the heat behind his eyes.

"See?" said the voice. "See what happens?"

"Little Bird!" Bee's voice hit the air too hard, as if she hadn't meant to shout.

Little Bird couldn't answer. He could only hold on and try to remember how to breathe.

Bee reached him in seconds, landing on the branch, wings trembling. "Are you hurt?"

Little Bird shook his head, not entirely sure. Everything hurt. And shame burned hotter than the bruises.

Bee settled close, not touching, just present. "That one hurt more than your body," she said.

"I chose it," Little Bird said, voice rough. "You didn't push me. I pushed myself. And I still fell."

They sat in the silence that follows a fall. Little Bird wanted to climb back up, hide in the nest, pretend he'd never tried. Something stubborn refused.

"Maybe I can't do this," he whispered.

Bee's wings drooped. For a moment, she looked very old.

"Maybe you can't," she said softly. "Or maybe you can and just haven't yet."

"What if I try again and fall again?"

"Then you'll fall again," Bee said simply. "And decide if it's worth another try."

Little Bird looked at the branch above them where he'd spent days learning to try. It seemed very far away. But they were just branches. He'd done harder things. He'd survived storms. He'd spoken honestly. He'd fallen and was still here.

"I'm going back up," Little Bird said.

Little Bird began to climb. Slowly, testing each foot placement. His wing hurt, but it worked. His chest ached, but it moved.

By the time he reached his branch, the sun was fully up.

"I could try a different branch," he said slowly. "Closer."

"You could," Bee said. "Or you could rest. There's no shame in resting."

Little Bird thought about it. His wing hurt. His shoulder hurt. Every part of him that had hit something during the fall was reminding him exactly where and how hard. Resting made sense.

But the moment of gliding still lived in his wings.

"There," he said, pointing with his beak to a nearer, lower branch. "That one."

Bee looked at the branch, then at him. "Are you sure?"

"No," Little Bird said honestly. "But I'm going to do it anyway."

"Then I'll watch," Bee said. "And if you fall again, we'll see what the wind was trying to teach."

Little Bird finished the climb back up, each move remembering the fall, shoulder protesting, wing stiff, but he kept going.

At the right height, he paused.

The next branch was close enough to hop, but that wasn't what he'd come for.

He wanted that moment again, the breath of air lifting him, wings catching it just right.

He stood at the edge, looking at the branch, he had chosen. This time, he didn't imagine success. He just looked where he meant to go and felt what his body wanted to do.

Wings spread. Air filled them. Gliding… Claws stretched. Gripping…

He stepped off.

The air found his wings, hello again, and he was gliding. His mind started up, what if, what if, but this time, he noticed and kept his attention on his wings.

Stay open. Feel the air. There's the branch.

His claws reached. Found. Gripped.

He wobbled, wings flapping hard for balance, but he held.

"Ha!" The sound burst out of him, half laugh, half disbelief.

Above him, Bee's hum lifted. "You did it!"

"I did it."

His whole body shook, torn between the effort of keeping his grip and the shock of nearly losing it.

Bee glided down to join him. "Worth it?"

"Yes."

They sat together on the lower branch, having reached it the hard way. The sun was higher now; the day warmed; the meadow busied itself with ordinary miracles.

"Tomorrow?" Bee asked.

Wind ran through Little Bird's feathers. "If the air invites me," he said.

Bee's hum softened. "You're close, Little Bird."

A breeze moved through the tree, carrying the smell of clover and distant rain. Little Bird spread his wings slightly, letting the air find their shape. Tomorrow, he'd try again. And the day after.

He looked at Bee, this old bee who kept sitting with him, even when he was frightened.

"Thank you," he said.

"For what?" Bee replied.

"For staying," Little Bird said. "Even when I dropped."

Bee's expression softened. "That's the easy part," she said. "The hard part was you getting back up."

CHAPTER FIVE

The Storm and the Still Point

The next day began in stillness.

The meadow was hushed, the sky heavy with waiting. Even the bees moved differently faster, lower, purposeful as if they knew something the air hadn't said yet. Bee arrived thoughtful, her hum carrying a hint of thunder.

"Storm coming," she said.

Little Bird glanced up. Clouds gathered, dark and heavy, folding into themselves, restless and alive.

"Will it be bad?" he asked.

Bee tilted her head, studying the sky with the attention of one who'd read weather for seasons longer than Little Bird had been alive. "Can't tell yet," she said. "Let's stay close to the trunk, just in case."

They moved along the branch toward the thick trunk, where the bark offered shelter and the branches knit together. Little Bird's heart was already racing, and the storm hadn't even arrived.

"I remember storms," he said quietly.

Bee settled beside him. "Most creatures do."

The wind began low and distant, a warning whispered across miles. The first gust touches Little Bird's feathers, gentle still, almost curious. But he knew what was coming.

Little Bird was practising holding his wings open against the wind when the memory hit him: his brother doing exactly this. But laughing. Finding it fun.

"You're thinking about him," Bee said. It wasn't a question.

Little Bird nodded, throat tight. "He would have loved this. The wind. The challenge. He thought everything was a game."

"What was he like?"

"Fearless," Little Bird said, and then paused.

"No. Not fearless. I think he was afraid… and he flew anyway. Mother used to say he never once turned back."

The wind gusted harder, pressing against Little Bird's wings. He trembled but held them steady.

"The morning, he died," Little Bird said quietly, "there was a storm coming. Everyone could see it. The sky was restless. Mother told us to stay in the nest. But he said he wanted to feel what storm-wind was like. Just for a moment. Just to know."

Bee's wings drooped.

"He jumped during a gust," Little Bird said, voice fading to almost nothing. "The wind caught him sideways, threw him against a branch. By the time he reached the ground, he was already gone."

"And you think you'll be like him," Bee said.

"What if there's no middle path?"

"There is," Bee said, moving closer. "You're on it."

Little Bird looked at her, then at the darkening sky. "This is his storm," he whispered. "This is the wind that killed him."

"Then we'll meet it together," Bee said. "And you'll meet it differently than he did."

The first wind came like a warning.

It rolled through the trees, long and low, the breath of something ancient. The birch swayed, branches creaking their wooden language. Little Bird's claws tightened.

"It's just wind," he told himself, but the wind wasn't listening.

Bee moved closer. No words, no wisdom, just presence: warm, solid, there.

The second gust hit harder, a shove instead of a touch. Leaves tore free and twirled away like frightened thoughts. The temperature dropped. Little Bird's feathers stood on end.

"Bee?" His voice came out thinner than he meant.

"I'm here."

The sky darkened quickly, swallowing the light. Across the valley, a grey wall of rain moved, hiding what it touched first the meadow, then the hills, then even the hive.

"This is what he saw," Little Bird thought. "This exact moment. Before the wind took him."

And then it reached them.

Rain hit like stones, cold, sharp, intent. Little Bird gasped, ducked his head under his wing, but water found him anyway, through feathers, down his back in icy streams. The wind came with it not the curious breath he'd begun to trust, not yesterday's friendly lift, but a gust with teeth.

It grabbed at him, trying to peel him from the branch, to tear him loose and throw him the way it had thrown his brother.

"Hold on!" Bee's voice, barely audible over the roar.

Little Bird held on. His claws dug so hard they might bleed. Storm. Memory. Body shaking before thought returned.

Lightning cracked the sky, brilliant, merciless. For one frozen moment, he saw everything: the meadow below, the ground where his brother had landed, the storm trying to make him fall the same way.

"He called for us," Little Bird gasped.

The wind swallowed most of his voice.

He hadn't meant to say it, but panic ripped it free.

"When he was falling. He called for us, and we couldn't help. We just watched."

Thunder drowned whatever came next. The whole tree shuddered, branches lashing as if to throw everything off every bird, every nest, every creature foolish enough to be caught.

Bee pressed against him, and Little Bird noticed the old bee trembled too. Even wisdom couldn't calm a storm.

"I don't know the right words," Bee said, voice rough.

"You don't have to say anything," Little Bird managed.
"

The wind hit again, harder. Little Bird's grip slipped, just enough to stop his heart. He scrambled for purchase, wings spreading instinctively for balance, giving the wind more to grab.

"Wings in!" Bee cried. "Fold close!"

Little Bird tried, but his wings wouldn't obey, caught in the wind, fighting it, trying to hold him steady and making it worse. He was going to fall, claws giving, wind swallowing his wings, the ground waiting the same way it had waited for his brother.

"Over here!" Bee's voice cut through the panic. "Look at me!"

Little Bird turned, rain streaming into his eyes.

Bee was there. Wings plastered to her sides, stripes running with water, antennae bent by wind, but there. Not flying away. Not leaving. Just there.

"Here," Bee said. One word. Steady. Real.

Wind howled. Rain fell. But for a moment: claws on bark, trunk at his back, someone staying.

The storm didn't care. It kept trying to shake them loose, throwing rain and wind and the memory of his brother's last moments. But Little Bird kept breathing. Kept holding on. Stayed here, not falling back to that day, not becoming that story.

Thunder and lightning came again, a crack that would surely split the tree. Little Bird flinched so hard he nearly lost his grip, but Bee's wing pressed against his side, just enough pressure to remind him where she was.

"We're still here," Bee said, wonder in her voice.

The wind shifted, not weaker, just different, coming from a new direction. The branch lurched. Suddenly, Little Bird was looking straight down at the distance that would kill him if he fell. His stomach twisted. His claws screamed.

He didn't let go.

"Move with it," he heard himself whisper. Not Bee's voice. His own.

He let his body sway, finding the branch's rhythm instead of fighting it. The motion was terrifying every shift, a fall beginning but it was better than rigidity, better than trying to be stronger than the tree itself.

Beside him, Bee made a small sound approval, maybe, or relief.

Time thinned. There was only wind, rain, holding on, breathing, the occasional flash that turned the world white. Little Bird's claws went numb. His waterlogged feathers made him feel twice as heavy. Every part of him hurt from holding on.

But he held on.

And slowly so slowly he almost didn't notice the wind began to tire. Rain softened from stones to drops. Gusts came farther apart. Lightning moved away, grumbling toward other trees.

Little Bird didn't relax right away. His body stayed clenched long after danger had moved on. Gradually, breath by breath, he let himself believe it: the storm was leaving and he remained.

When the rain finally stopped really stopped the silence felt too loud. He'd grown so used to the roar that quiet seemed like something waiting to return.

But the sky was lighter. Clouds broke apart, drifting east to frighten some other forest. Through the gaps, he saw blue actual blue as if the sky remembered its colour.

"We made it," Bee said, her voice hollowed out.

Little Bird nodded, not trusting his voice yet.

They sat in the dripping quiet, watching the world remember itself. The meadow emerged, dented and flattened in places, but there. The hive stood golden, somehow cheerful. Birds called tentatively, checking on each other, announcing survival.

"I thought" Little Bird started, then stopped.

"I know," Bee said.

"He shouted for us," Little Bird said anyway, needing to say it. "My brother. When the wind took him. We heard him and couldn't help. We just watched him fall."

Bee's antennae lowered. "I'm sorry."

"I thought I'd fall the same way," Little Bird whispered. "That the storm would take me too."

"But it didn't," Bee said.

"The storm's gone," Little Bird said. "But the fear stayed."

“Mine did, too,” Bee said. “My wings still tremble from the first lightning. I kept thinking: what if I can’t hold on? What if I fall? What if I’m too old for storms now?”

He saw Bee then, truly saw her. “You stayed anyway,” he said.

“So did you.”

They sat with that truth between them.

“I didn’t fall,” Little Bird said, almost in disbelief.

Little Bird spread his wings slightly, letting the sun begin the long work of drying them. They were heavy, waterlogged, but intact. He was intact. Scared, exhausted, whole.

“Tomorrow,” Bee said, “we practise again. The long flight is coming soon.”

Little Bird’s stomach dropped.

The storm had pushed everything else away. Only briefly.

The mountains were still out there. The wide water too. The places where there was nothing to land on if he fell.

"I'm not ready," he whispered.

"Maybe not," Bee said. "But you're more ready than yesterday."

"The storm was worse than flying," he said, testing the thought.

"Much worse," Bee agreed.

"And I made it through."

"You did. Not his way. Yours."

Little Bird looked out at the still-terrifying valley. It was possible.

"Will you stay while I keep trying?" he asked. "When I go higher… farther?"

Bee's eyes softened, storm-light catching in them. "I'll be here," she said. "Until your wings remember everything they need to know."

They sat as the afternoon turned gold, the forest drying, settling, forgiving the storm for passing through.

The wind rose again, gentle now instead of cruel. It touched Little Bird's damp feathers, and he didn't flinch. He acknowledged it, let it pass.

CHAPTER SIX

Dreaming of Sky

Evening settled over the branches.

The storm had rinsed the colour from everything the leaves, the grass, the air and now it all glowed faintly beneath a pale sky. The branch where Little Bird perched was still damp but steady. Beneath him, droplets slid down leaves like glass beads, catching the fading light.

Bee arrived slower than usual, wings heavy from rain, but her hum carried warmth.

"You stayed," she said simply.

Little Bird nodded. "I did. I was scared, and I stayed."

They sat for a while, the silence between them comfortable and full. The forest settled, unmaking the stormwater dripping, leaves settling, small creatures edging out from where they'd hidden.

“During the storm,” Bee said after a while. “What found you?”

Little Bird frowned. “Nothing. Everything was too fast wind, rain, and a memory that clung like cold feathers.”

“Mm,” Bee murmured, wings folding close.

Little Bird waited. But Bee only watched the valley, where mist gathered in the hollows as if the storm had left pieces of itself behind.

“My hive,” she said at last, voice low, “we used to sit at the entrance before the long flights before the light came and the world warmed.” Her hum thinned into a small laugh. “Cold enough you could almost see a bee breathe.”

She wasn’t looking at Little Bird anymore; she was far away, somewhere in another season.

“The old ones would sit with us. Just sit.” She paused. “They spoke of how the air would feel so the sky wouldn’t seem like a stranger.”

Little Bird leaned closer.

"One of the old bees had the softest hum." Bee's smile turned wistful. "She'd close her eyes and tell the morning: how the clover field shimmers when the sun first finds it; how the air pinches cold by the stream and loosens warm over the south meadow until a stray updraft catches you and the sky remembers you belong to it."

Bee's gaze flicked back to Little Bird storm-weary and gentle.

"When morning came," Bee said, "we'd fly. " And somehow the sky felt less strange.

"Did it help?"

"A little," Bee said. "Enough to try."

The light was fading faster now, the sky deepening from gold to rose to something closer to purple. The temperature drop: his feathers fluffed against the coming cold.

"I've been trying to imagine flying," Little Bird admitted. "But when I do, I just see falling."

Bee tilted her head. "What else do you see?"

Little Bird closed his eyes. The images came: the ground rushing up, wings forgetting, the moment of impact.

"The ground," he whispered. "Always the ground."

"Just the ground?"

Little Bird opened his eyes. "What else would there be?"

Bee's voice softened. "When I was young younger than I am now I was terrified of crossing water. Rivers, streams, even big puddles. I'd fly out of my way to avoid them."

"Why?"

My brother fell into a river," she said. "The current was faster than his wings." Her voice carried old grief, worn smooth by years. "After that, every time I saw water, I thought of him."

Little Bird recognised this. "What changed?"

"There was an old bee once," she said, her voice going warm around the edges. "She found me by a stream I was too scared to cross."

She looked down, as if the stream might still be there beneath them.

'She sat with me a long while, hardly spoke, just noticed things.' She smiled. 'She looked at the far bank and say, "That willow. Notice the far bank. Imagine arriving. Imagine belonging there."'

Bee's eyes flicked to where the sky met the land.

'Then she'd look at the water. "It catches the light," she'd whisper. "Imagine being high enough that the shimmer is all you see no danger, just a ribbon of bright sky lying down."'

Her wings gave a small, remembering twitch.

"Somehow," she said, "that made the air feel a little closer. Like it could hold me."

"Did you fly across?"

"Not that day," she said. "But I went back, morning after morning, picturing it the landing on the willow, the height where water looked like light, the feel of arriving on the far side." She paused. "And then one morning, I didn't think about it. I just flew."

The evening had grown still around them, as if the forest were listening too.

Little Bird gazed across the valley. The mist was thicker now, turning the meadow into something dreamlike and distant. He tried to imagine crossing it not falling but flying and for a moment he could almost feel the air underneath, his wings catching and pulling, the world below growing small and strange and bright.

Then the image vanished, wiped out by the sudden tightening of everything inside him.

"It slipped," he murmured.

"It comes and goes. Like the wind." Bee said.

They sat in silence as the first stars pushed through the clearing sky. Little Bird's body softened the kind that happens when you stop pretending to be strong.

"Tell me what it's like," Little Bird asked. "Flying."

Bee's hum drifted low. "Close your eyes."

And Little Bird saw it, not a picture but a pull. Air widening, branch falling away, wings finding space. Effortless. Movement.

Then night again.

Bee was watching him. “You saw it.”

He nodded.

The night breeze arrived, carrying the scent of wet earth and new beginnings.

“Bee?” Little Bird asked. “Do you still imagine flights? Even now?”

Her expression shifted something vulnerable crossing her face. “Every night,” she said. “ Flights that live only in memory.” She paused. “But also new things. Tomorrow’s flowers. Next season’s sun. The moment you finally trust the sky enough to meet it.”

Little Bird’s throat tightened. “You imagine my flight?”

“Every night,” she said. “I’ve watched your wings grow surer in my mind.”

They sat until darkness deepened two creatures who’d found each other when they needed finding. The forest breathed around them, settling, resting, dreaming its own dreams.

Bee flexed her wings. "Tomorrow," she said, "you won't need to imagine it."

Little Bird met her gaze. "I'm ready."

"I know," Bee said. "You showed me."

She lifted into the darkness, her hum fading until it was just another sound the night made.

Little Bird pressed himself against the trunk, closed his eyes, and let the flight return.

This time, he flew.

CHAPTER SEVEN

Where the Wind Knows Your Name

Morning arrived in the hush that follows a storm

The air was soft again, the sky freshly washed.

Every leaf gleamed, as if the night had wiped the world clean.

Little Bird woke before the sun fully rose, his feathers smooth, his eyes open and ready for what came next.

Bee was already there, sitting on the same branch, humming quietly to herself.

“You’re early,” she said.

“So are you,” said Little Bird.

They sat in silence, watching the valley wake. The mist was thin today, more suggestion than barrier. Through it, Little Bird could see the meadow clearly, every flower, every blade of grass, the path he'd walked with Bee days ago that had seemed so impossibly far.

A long moment passed. A woodpecker worked somewhere in the canopy above them steady, purposeful, the sound of someone who knew exactly what they were doing. Little Bird listened, wishing his own wings felt that sure.

"I flew it in my sleep," Little Bird said. "Sometimes I landed, sometimes I didn't. But I kept trying."

Bee's antennae lifted. "And when you didn't?"

"I woke up," Little Bird said. "Then I'd fall asleep again and fly it differently."

They watched the sun climb higher, turning the mist golden. Somewhere below, the hive was already humming, awake before everything else.

Little Bird stood, moving toward the edge almost without deciding to. His claws found the familiar grooves in the bark, the places worn smooth by his pacing. The wind rose to meet him, gentle today, almost encouraging.

Bee watched but didn't speak.

Little Bird spread his wings, feeling the air find them, finding their shape. He'd done this so many times now. But this time was different.

He looked down. The ground was far. Not as far as it used to seem, but far enough to hurt.

Careful, whispered a familiar voice.

"I remember," Little Bird said.

And you think you're different?

"I don't know."

He stepped back from the edge, breath coming fast.

Bee tilted her head. "The sky won't run away."

But even as he stepped back, his wings twitched. Wanting.

He paced along the branch, agitated... A few steps toward the trunk, a few steps back toward the edge.

"What if I wait too long?" Little Bird asked suddenly. "What if the flock leaves and I'm still here, still afraid?"

Bee's hum deepened. "Then you'll find another way south," she said. "Or you'll stay. I don't know. Not every question has an answer."

He moved to the edge again. This time faster, before he could stop himself. The wind gusted, not hard, just sudden, and his wings opened without thought, catching air.

For a heartbeat, he was lifted. Actually lifted, his claws leaving bark, his body suspended by nothing but wind and feather and the wild hope that this could work.

Then panic seized him, *this is it, this is how falling starts*, and his wings forgot everything. They clamped shut. His body dropped.

The world tilted sickeningly. He scrambled for the branch, missed, and tumbled through the leaves. Branches slapped at him, his wing, his chest, his head, everything too fast and off balance.

He crashed into the trunk halfway down, the impact punching the air from his lungs. His claws found bark on instinct, and he clung there, gasping, everything spinning.

"Little Bird!" Bee's voice came out too sharp, sharper than she meant.

He couldn't answer. Couldn't move. His breath stayed high and thin.

Bee reached him quickly, landing beside him on the trunk. "Are you hurt?"

Little Bird shook his head, though he wasn't entirely sure. His wing ached where he'd clipped a branch. His chest throbbed.

Worse than any of that was Bee's face worry and guilt tangled together.

"I wanted it for you," she said.

"I wanted to try," Little Bird managed.

They sat together in the silence after the fall. Little Bird wanted to climb back to the nest, to hide under his mother's wing, to forget he'd ever thought he could do this. But something stubborn in him refused.

"Maybe I can't do this," he whispered.

"Maybe not," Bee said. "Or maybe you can and just haven't yet." She held Little Bird's gaze. "I don't know which is true. But you'll fall, and then you'll have to decide if it's worth trying again," she reminded him.

Little Bird began climbing. Slowly, testing each foot placement. His wing hurt, but it worked. His chest ached, but it moved. By the time he reached his branch, the sun was fully up.

He stood at the edge once more.

This time, he didn't look at Bee for reassurance or permission. He just looked at the space ahead.

What happened? he asked himself. *Before the fear?*

He closed his eyes.

The wind under his wings.

The sudden weightlessness.

Joy before panic swallowed it.

He opened his wings.

Pushed off.

And dropped.

The air rushed past his face, cold and fast and too much like *that* day, the drop, the speed, the helpless plummet toward the meadow where his brother hit the ground and didn't get up.

His wings snapped wide

and he was still falling

the ground getting closer, the meadow sharpening from blur into detail, he could see individual grass stems now, could see the stones, the exact place where he would hit

his chest seized, his mind screamed pull up, pull up, pull up, PULL UP

his wings beat once, desperate, uncontrolled, flailing at the air as if it was an enemy

he dropped lower, the flowers getting closer, he could smell them now, the clover and the wild grass and the earth underneath

his wings beat again, wild, panicked

but something was different.

The air.

It had weight. It had shape. It had texture.

It was pushing back.

Not enough. Still falling, but less. Falling more slowly.

His wings beat again, and this time, he didn't think about what his wings should do, didn't try to remember Bee's advice, didn't analyse the angle of his feathers or the position of his body, his body just knew.

Something clicked.

Something locked into place.

The falling stopped.

Not gradually. Suddenly. Between one wingbeat and the next, he went from falling to...

Not falling.

He hung there, suspended between ground and sky, between terror and steady rhythm, and the air was holding him, actually holding him.

This is it, he thought. This is flying.

The wind against his feathers, each one finding its angle. The cool pressure held him up. His shoulders worked, aching, but stronger than he'd been before."

The burn in his chest muscles, fierce and good. Pain that meant function. Pain that meant power.

He wasn't graceful.

His wingbeats were uneven right wing pulling harder than left, his body tilting, overcorrecting. The wind found every mistake in his form and pushed at it, tested it.

But he was up.

The meadow dropped away beneath him. Higher. Higher still. Higher than he'd been since leaving the nest. Higher than he'd ever been under his own power.

He could see everything now:

The stream, silver and winding, cutting through the green landscape. Fish shadows sliding underneath. Stones breaking the water into small rapids where the current ran fast.

The patch of clover where Bee worked, and. where the other bees moved in their systematic patterns, gathering what they needed to survive another day. The hive in the distance, golden in the morning light, humming with thousands of small bodies working side by side.

The valley spread below him, familiar but remade. From the ground, the meadow was overwhelming too much grass, too many flowers, too much space. From up here, it formed a pattern. It made sense. It had shape.

His wings burned.

The ache had gone from fierce to steady. He'd been flying how long? Time had folded in on itself.

But his wings were done. They'd given him what they had.

Time to land.

He circled back toward the tree, wingbeats less steady now, fatigue making everything harder.

The branch appeared below him his branch, Bee's branch, where this had all started.

He aimed for it.

Not the way he meant to.

His angle was too steep. His speed was too fast. His approach was too high, a landing attempted with the graceless enthusiasm of someone who'd never landed before.

The branch rushed at him too fast, too close, too solid.

He tried to slow down, overcorrected, and tilted sideways.

His wings flared wide, trying to brake, catching too much air, pushing him off course.

He hit the branch hard in more of a controlled crash than a landing. His claws scrabbled for purchase, sliding on bark, wings wild and uncoordinated, his whole body trying to find grip and failing, then trying again.

For a terrible moment, he thought he'd bounce off entirely, tumble all the way down, crash through branches back to the ground where he'd started.

But his claws found bark.

Dug in.

Held.

And he was there. Standing. On the same branch he'd left.

His legs shook. His wings trembled. His breath came in ragged gasps.

Bee was beside him. The old bee's wings were trembling too.

"Well," Bee said, her voice rough. "You were in the sky."

Little Bird couldn't speak, throat too tight, chest heaving, every part of him shaking.

Everything hurt. Wings, chest, legs weak and trembling. His whole body screamed that he'd pushed too hard, gone too far.

"I flew," he managed finally, his voice cracking on the word.

"You did," Bee nodded.

"I fell first."

"You did," Bee agreed. "And then you flew anyway."

Little Bird found himself looking out across the valley the same view he'd been staring at for weeks, the same meadow, the same stream, the same sky. But different now. Because he'd been out there. In it. Part of it, instead of just watching it.

"Tomorrow," Little Bird said, steadier now, "I'll try again. And the day after. Until it feels less like falling."

"And more like flying," Bee said.

"Yes."

The sun climbed higher. Somewhere in the distance, the flock called to each other, practising their formations, preparing for the long flight south. Little Bird listened and knew he would join them.

Not today. Not tomorrow. But soon.

He looked at Bee, this old bee who had sat with him when he was frightened.

"Thank you," Little Bird said.

Bee shook her head. "I stayed. But you flew."

"You stayed," Little Bird said. "That helped."

They sat until the warmth had baked into their wings and the day was fully awake. Until Little Bird's heartbeat had returned to normal and the shaking in his legs had subsided.

Until the moment felt less like a miracle and more like something that had happened something that could happen again.

When Bee finally rose to leave, her hum sounded different lighter somehow, younger.

Little Bird watched her go, watched the old bee drift back toward the meadow where flowers waited, and the hive hummed as it always had.

He spread his wings one more time, just to feel them.

They trembled from the work they'd done.

But they were his.

And they worked.

Tomorrow, he would fly again.

EPILOGUE

The Day the Sky Called

That morning came too soon.

Little Bird had known it would. The season had been moving toward this day slowly and surely. The blackberries had softened and fallen. The winds had turned south. Yesterday, the flock had gathered in the high meadow, circling and calling with that old, urgent cry that meant *it was time.*

Bee arrived before dawn. She carried nothing, no nectar, no new wordsonly herself. She settled on the branch one last time.

"Today," Little Bird said.

"Today," Bee agreed.

They sat together in the grey light, watching the valley wake.

"Are you ready?" Bee asked at last.

Little Bird laughed a dry, breathless sound. "No. But I'm going anyway."

Bee smiled faintly. "Yes."

From the meadow, the flock called again. Little Bird saw them now: dark shapes against a whitening sky, circling, waiting for the stragglers, the frightened, the first timers.

His mother landed beside him, eyes soft. She didn't speak. She touched his wing with her beak, once, gently, then lifted toward the gathering flock.

"She's not waiting," Little Bird said, barely above a whisper.

"She knows you'll find her," Bee said.

Little Bird stared down at the branch. Every scratch in the bark was familiar. Every curve was home.

"I don't know if I can do this," he whispered.

Bee's wings shifted slightly, catching the pale light. "No one ever really knows," she said. "We just go when the wind insists."

The flock called again, sharper now. The wind was right. The day was already pulling away from him.

Little Bird stepped toward the edge, his body already knowing what came next.

"Bee…" The rest of the words wouldn't come.

Bee's wings lifted slightly. "You don't have to," she said. "I know."

He opened his wings. The air met him, familiar and kind.

"Come back next spring." Bee said, "Tell me about the warm shores."

"I will," Little Bird promised.

The flock was leaving now no longer calling, just going. A river of wings flowing south toward warmth and whatever waited beyond distance.

His mother's voice rose once more. *Come. Come now.*

Little Bird glanced at Bee one last time this old bee who had stopped to sit with a frightened bird.

“Fly well, Little Bird,” Bee said.

And Little Bird stepped off the branch.

His wings opened. The air caught him, lifted him. He rose toward the flock, toward his mother’s voice, toward the south and the wide sky. He circled once, just once.

Below, Bee stood on the branch, smaller now, wings lifted.

Then Little Bird turned south and was gone into the bright air.

Bee stayed long after the last shape disappeared. The morning warmed around her. The meadow went on: flowers opening, mice foraging, spiders repairing the night’s damage.

She could have gone back to the hive there was always work but she stayed.

After a while, she noticed something caught in the bark where Little Bird had stood: a small feather, white and soft, light enough to vanish in the next serious wind.

Bee touched it gently with one leg.

She wedged it into a crack in the bark where the wind couldn't reach.

"Fly well," she whispered to the empty air. "Fly well, Little Bird."

Next spring, she would come to this branch again, just in case.

Hoping.

The day warmed. Bees worked. The sky went on being sky. Bee hummed low, almost to herself, and flew for home.

Author's Note

Sometimes confidence disappears quietly.

Not because we failed, or did something wrong, or weren't strong enough, but because life asked more of us than we had to give in that moment. Fear grows roots. Grief settles in our bones. And before we notice it happening, the sky we used to rise into with ease begins to feel impossibly far away.

I wrote *Little Bird* during a season when I was helping people find their way back to themselves not by ignoring fear, but by understanding it. Not by becoming fearless, but by learning to move again with shaking wings.

This story is simple on the surface, but it carries truths I've seen in every kind of person: professionals, parents, leaders, teenagers, people under pressure, people rebuilding. We are all Little Bird at some point. And we all need a Bee someone steady enough to sit beside us until our own strength reappears.

If this story found you at the right moment, I'm glad you're here.

J.M. Walsh

About the Author

J.M. Walsh is a writer, leadership mentor, and confidence specialist who has spent more than two decades helping people navigate fear, pressure, uncertainty, and change. His work is rooted in behavioural psychology, emotional resilience, and the quiet strength found in everyday courage.

He is trained as an Adult Educator, a Clinical Hypnotherapist, and a Master Practitioner of NLP, blending science, story, and practical tools to help people build confidence from the inside out.

Little Bird is his first fable a gentle story for anyone beginning again.

He lives in the United Kingdom and writes books, programmes, and tools for people who want to live, lead, and work with calm, grounded confidence.

Also, by J.M. Walsh

The Confidence Under Pressure Series

Unshakeable Confidence
A practical guide to rebuilding real, grounded confidence even when life feels overwhelming.

The Confident Life
How to design and live a life that strengthens your confidence every day.

Unthinkable Confidence
A deeper exploration of courage, high performance, and becoming the person, you know you can be.

Nervous, Not Broken
Understanding anxiety, and learning the difference between what is natural and what needs care.

More titles coming soon.

If Little Bird's journey spoke to you...

I would love to stay connected.

You can find more books, articles, programmes, and resources on building calm, grounded confidence at:

www.breakthroughchange.com

Your review also makes a meaningful difference.

If you have a moment to share your thoughts on Amazon, it helps this story reach someone who may need it.

Thank you for reading.

Acknowledgements

Thank you to the people who encouraged this story into existence those who listened, reflected, and reminded me of the quiet strength that lives inside all of us.

To everyone who has shared their own fears, doubts, and moments of courage with me over the years, thank you. Your stories shaped this one.

And to the early readers and supporters who believed in *Little Bird* long before it reached its final form your kindness matters more than you know.